Cows

A Level Two Reader

By Cynthia Klingel and Robert B. Noyed

The
Child's
World®

Cows make a "moo" sound.
They have four legs and a
long tail. Some cows have
horns, too.

Cows are large animals. Some cows are black and white. Others are black, brown, or tan.

Most cows live on farms.

Some cows stay in barns.

Others live in fields.

Male cows are called bulls.

Female cows are called cows.

Female cows produce milk.

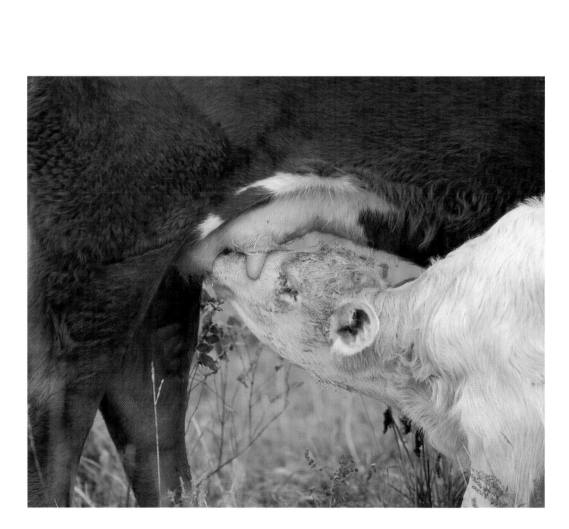

A baby cow is called a calf.
A calf drinks its mother's
milk until it is about six
months old.

Cows eat plant foods. They eat dried grass called hay. Cows also eat oats and corn.

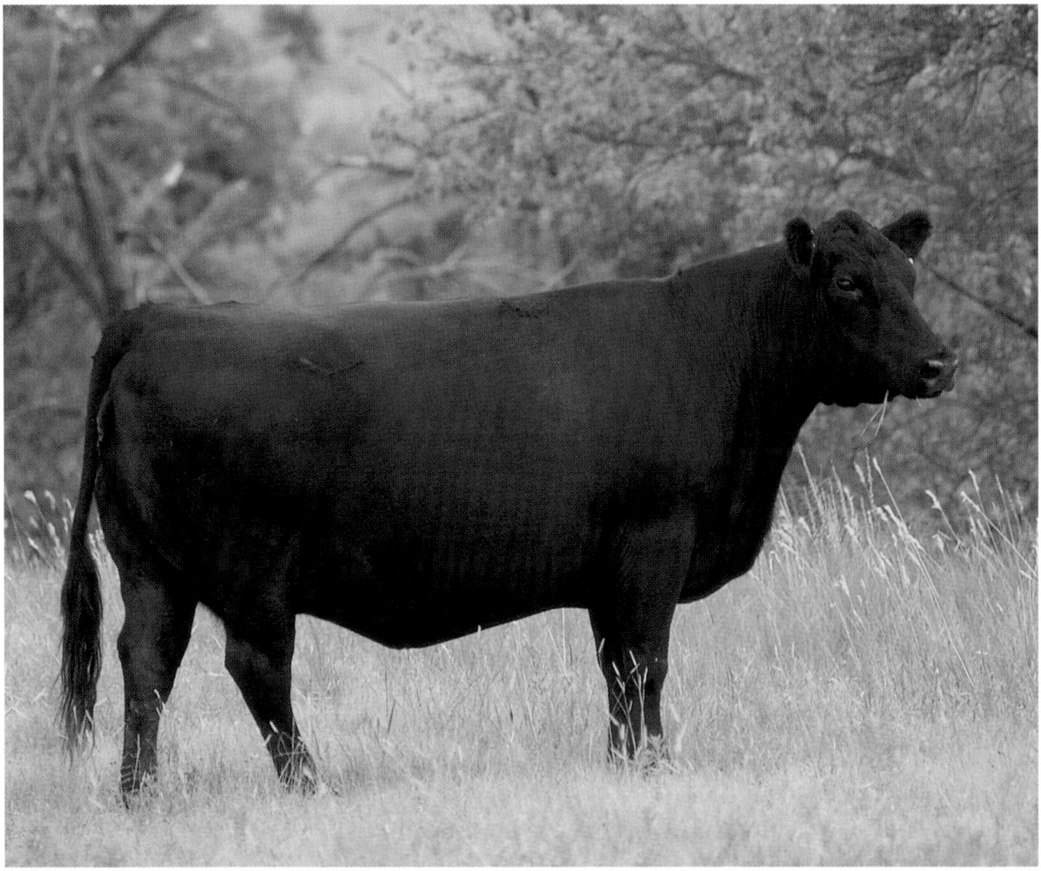

Cows are raised for many reasons. We eat the meat that comes from cows. This meat is called beef.

Dairy cows give milk. We drink cows' milk. Ice cream, yogurt, and cheese are made from milk.

Skins from cows are called hides. Leather is made from cowhides. This leather is used to make shoes, belts, and clothing.

Cows give many things to people. They are very important animals.

21

Index

To Find Out More

Books

Aliki. *Milk from Cow to Carton.* New York: HarperCollins, 1992.

Kalman, Bobbie. *Hooray for Dairy Farming!* New York: Crabtree Pub. Co., 1998.

McDonald, Mary Ann. *Cows.* Chanhassen, Minn.: The Child's World, 1998.

Web Sites

Cows of the World
http://www.tc.umn.edu/~puk/cow/cowworld.html
An alphabetical listing of the more than 900 cattle breeds from around the world.

Straus Family Creamery: Kid's Page
http://www.strausmilk.com/kids.htm
Information about making butter and milking cows.

Note to Parents and Educators

Welcome to The Wonders of Reading™! These books provide text at three different levels for beginning readers to practice and strengthen their reading skills. Additionally, the use of nonfiction text provides readers the valuable opportunity to *read to learn*, not just to learn to read.

These leveled readers allow children to choose books at their level of reading confidence and performance. Level One books offer beginning readers simple language, word choice, and sentence structure as well as a word list. Level Two books feature slightly more difficult vocabulary, longer sentences, and longer total text. In the back of each Level Two book are an index and a list of books and Web sites for finding out more information. Level Three books continue to extend word choice and length of text. In the back of each Level Three book are a glossary, an index, and a list of books and Web sites for further research.

State and national standards in reading and language arts emphasize using nonfiction at all levels of reading development. The Wonders of Reading™ fill the historical void in nonfiction material for the primary grade readers with the additional benefit of a leveled text.

About the Authors

Cindy Klingel has worked as a high school English teacher and an elementary teacher. She is currently the curriculum director for a Minnesota school district. Writing children's books is another way for her to continue her passion for sharing the written word with children. Cindy Klingel is a frequent visitor to the children's section of bookstores and enjoys spending time with her many friends, family, and two daughters.

Bob Noyed started his career as a newspaper reporter. Since then, he has worked in communications and public relations for more than fourteen years for a Minnesota school district. He enjoys writing books for children and finds that it brings a different feeling of challenge and accomplishment from other writing projects. He is an avid reader who also enjoys music, theater, traveling, and spending time with his wife, son, and daughter.

Published by The Child's World®, Inc.
PO Box 326
Chanhassen, MN 55317-0326
800-599-READ
www.childsworld.com

Photo Credits
© Barry Lewis/Tony Stone Images: 9
© Eric R. Berndt/Unicorn Stock Photos: 10
© Flanagan Publishing Services/Romie Flanagan: 18
© Frank Siteman/PhotoEdit: 21
© Graeme Norways/Tony Stone Images: 17
© James P. Rowan: 2, 14
© Peter Cade/Tony Stone Images: 5
© Tim Davis/Tony Stone Images: cover
© Tony Craddock/Tony Stone Worldwide: 6
© Tony Stone Worldwide: 13

Project Coordination: Editorial Directions, Inc.
Photo Research: Alice K. Flanagan

Library of Congress Cataloging-in-Publication Data
Klingel, Cynthia Fitterer.
Cows / by Cynthia Klingel and Robert B. Noyed.
p. cm. — (Wonder books)
Summary: A simple introduction to the physical characteristics and behavior of cows.
ISBN 1-56766-820-8 (alk. paper)
1. Cows—Juvenile literature. 2. Cattle—Juvenile literature. [1. Cows.]
I. Noyed, Robert B.   II. Title.   III. Wonder books (Chanhassen, Minn.)

SF197.5 .K65   2000
636.2—dc21   99-057843

24